THE BROTHERS

REWRITTEN BY ELIZABETH LANE
ILLUSTRATED BY BRENDEN TAYLOR

In the ancient land of Israel, a man named Eli lived with his two sons. The boys were named Samuel and Joshua, and they were always together.

In the fall when the first rains came, Samuel and Joshua helped their father plow the land. They helped him plant the wheat that fed their family.

As the wheat grew, Samuel and Joshua guarded it from the birds. Sometimes they played games among the tall wheat stalks. But they were always careful not to trample the wheat.

When the wheat was golden, Eli cut the long stalks with a sickle. Samuel and Joshua helped bundle the wheat stalks into sheaves. They tied the sheaves to the donkey and took the wheat to the threshing floor.

Samuel and Joshua helped spread the wheat on the threshing floor. Then Samuel rode the donkey around and around the threshing floor while Joshua rode behind on the sledge. The sledge and the donkey's hooves separated the kernels of wheat from the stalks.

Samuel and Joshua helped to toss the wheat into the air so that the breeze could carry away the chaff. It was Samuel and Joshua who sang the loudest and danced the most when, at last, the precious grains of wheat were stored away in the large clay jars.

As the years passed, Samuel and Joshua grew to be men. Eli, their father, grew to be old. Before he died, he gave half his land to Samuel and half to Joshua. “Always take care of the land,” their father said. “And always remember: It is good when brothers live together in friendship.”

Joshua married a lovely woman named Sarah, and with Samuel's help, built a house on his own land. As time passed, they had three children. Samuel did not get married. He lived in his father's house alone.

One winter there was almost no rain. The hot, yellow sun baked the earth. Only a little wheat grew on Samuel's land. Only a little wheat grew on Joshua's land. Both brothers worried as they carried the sheaves to their threshing floors. Would there be enough wheat to last until the next harvest?

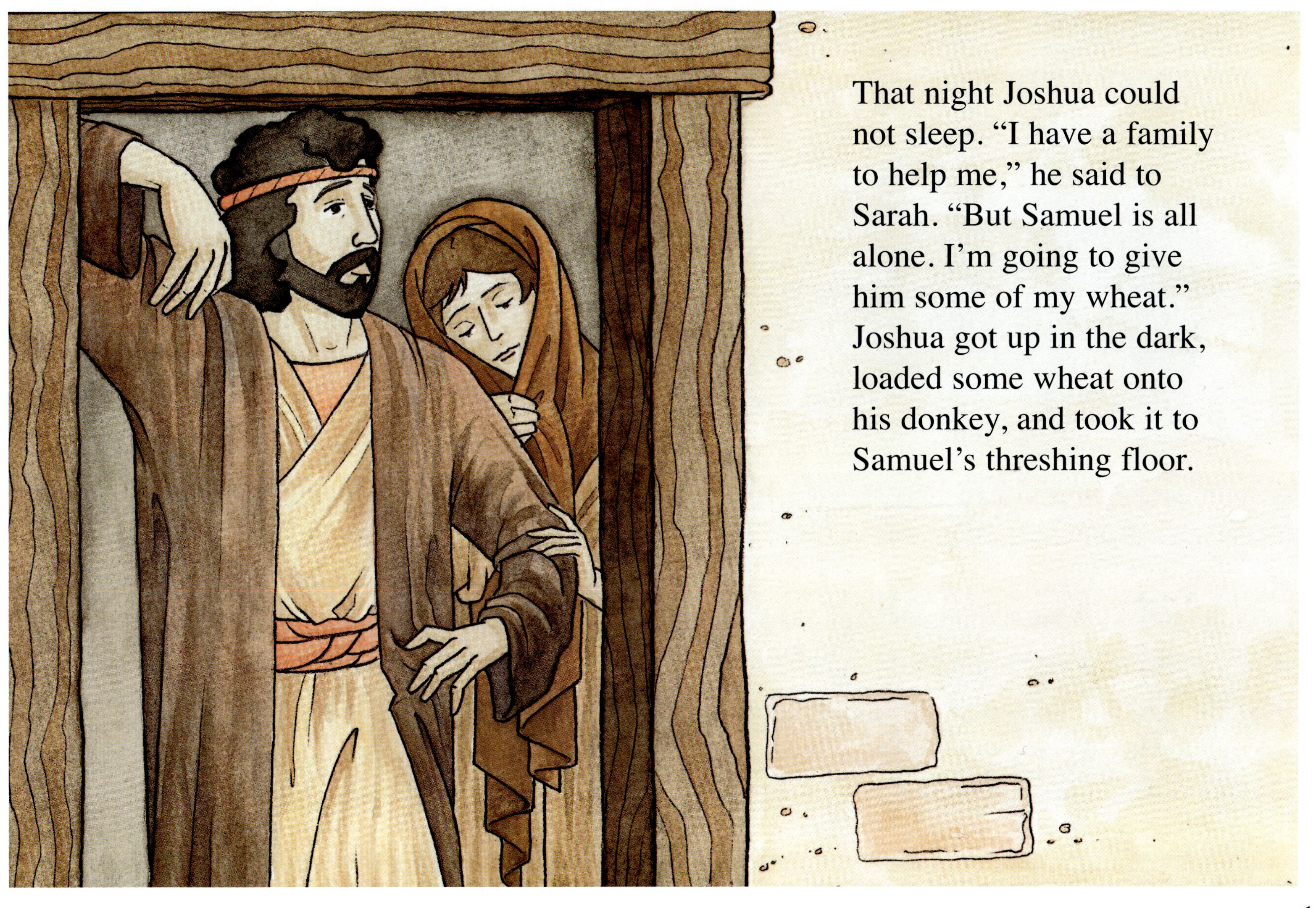

That night Joshua could not sleep. "I have a family to help me," he said to Sarah. "But Samuel is all alone. I'm going to give him some of my wheat." Joshua got up in the dark, loaded some wheat onto his donkey, and took it to Samuel's threshing floor.

That night Samuel could not sleep either. “My brother has a wife and children to feed,” he said to himself. “He needs more wheat than I do. I’m going to give him some of my wheat.” Samuel got up in the dark, loaded some wheat onto his donkey, and took it to Joshua’s threshing floor.

The next morning, Joshua saw that he had as much wheat as before. “I didn’t give my brother enough,” he said. “Tonight I will take him more wheat.”

Samuel also saw that he had as much wheat as before. “I didn’t give my brother enough,” he said. “Tonight I will take him more wheat.”

That night Joshua loaded more wheat onto his donkey and took it to Samuel's threshing floor. Samuel loaded more wheat onto his donkey and took it to Joshua's threshing floor. They passed in the dark without seeing each other.

The next morning, each brother had as much wheat as before. "Tonight I must take more wheat to my brother," said Joshua. "The children and I will help you," said Sarah.

That night Joshua loaded his donkey with wheat. Sarah and the children gathered up all the wheat they could carry. They all set out for Samuel's threshing floor.

Samuel was taking more wheat to his brother when
he saw Joshua's family coming across the field.
He dropped the wheat and ran to meet them.

As the two brothers hugged
each other, they heard in their
hearts a voice singing:
"It is good when brothers live
together in friendship."

Hundreds of years passed, and where the brothers' fields used to be, a city grew up—the city of Jerusalem. On the place where the brothers had met and hugged each other in the night, King Solomon built the Holy Temple.

When the temple was finished, everyone heard in their hearts a voice singing: "It is good when all people live together in friendship."